INSIDE THE CIRCUS

WRITTEN AND ILLUSTRATED
BY FRANK FITZGERALD

A CALICO BOOK

Published by Contemporary Books, Inc.

CHICAGO · NEW YORK

Library of Congress Cataloging-in-Publication Data

Fitzgerald, Frank.
Inside the circus / written and illustrated by Frank Fitzgerald
p.   cm.
"A Calico book."
Summary: Max and his grandfather visit the circus, where they see
every aspect from putting up the Big Top to spending the night in
the manager's trailer.
ISBN 0-8092-4359-8
[1. Circus—Fiction.]   I. Title.
PZ7.F574In   1989

[E]—dc19   88-35039
                                                                              CIP
                                                                              AC

To little people and big people and the good planet Earth
—FF

Thanks to the Carson and Barnes Circus, especially D. R. Miller,
Jim Judson, Ken Holehouse, and Donna Milson. Also Robert
Parkinson, Bill McCarthy, Fred Pfening, Jr., Fred Powledge,
John and Alice Durant, Timothy Germany, Candice Coram, Leonard
Burg, Matthew Weingardt, and M. J. Pashley. Their help in preparing
this book is greatly appreciated.

It was 6:30 in the morning—early for Max to be up. But this was a special day. The circus was coming to town!

Max and his Grandpa Sam were going to watch the circus set up. Max's grandfather had once worked as a ringmaster for the Boone-Rissler Circus. "Here it comes, Grandpa!" yelled Max as the first trucks rolled into sight.

When they reached the lot, Grandpa Sam explained, "Not all circuses are the same. The tents and equipment and the way things are done can be very different." Then he told Max what each person and machine in this circus did.

"There's Roy," said Grandpa. "He's called the twenty-four-hour man. He travels one day ahead of the circus to find the best route to the circus lot. Then he puts up arrows for the others to follow."

"That truck over there with the noisy machine on the back is called a stake driver," Grandpa Sam told Max. "It's hammering stakes into the ground. The circus-tent ropes will be tied to those stakes after the tent is put up."

4

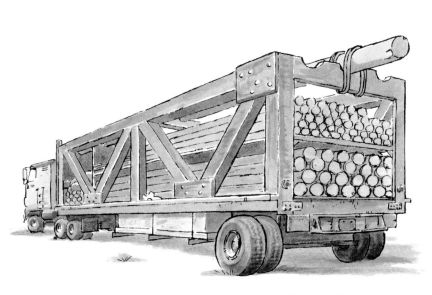

Max watched the pole truck pull up. It hauled the long poles that hold up the tent.

Max and Grandpa Sam walked past another huge truck. "This truck provides the electric power for the circus," Sam explained.

When the cook house arrived, the cooks wasted no time getting ready to feed the workers.

Max didn't know so much was needed to make a circus happen. "Look over there, Max," Grandpa Sam said. "Here come the animals!"

Many of the circus animals were transported in trucks. "Some of the animals are tied to railings inside so that they won't roam around and get hurt while the truck is moving," said Grandpa Sam.

Other animals were moved in cages.

Some performers brought their own animals. The Amazing Alfredo kept Snoopy, his snake, in the shower of his motor home.

6

Mr. Hanbury made a special cage in the back seat of his station wagon for his monkey, Chi Chi.

The workers who set up the circus lived in sleeper trailers.

"Most of the performers live in motor homes or campers," said Grandpa Sam. "An acrobat family, the Bouncing Barretts, made a traveling home out of a bus.

"Let's go watch them put up the tent," said Grandpa Sam. "A tent circus like this one is sometimes called a mud show," he explained. "It is set up outdoors, so the crew has to work in the mud if it rains."

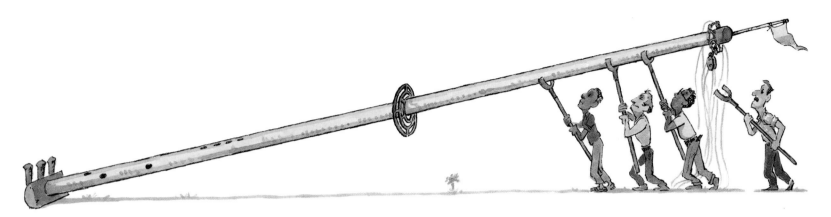

"Look, Max," exclaimed Grandpa Sam, "the workers are just beginning to put up the center pole. That's the main support of the tent. See the ring on the pole? That's called a bale ring. The tent will be attached to that ring as soon as the pole is raised."

After the workers pushed the center pole up as far as they could, Rosie the elephant took over. She was harnessed to a rope that was hooked to the center pole. Slowly Rosie moved forward, pulling the pole until it stood straight up. Then other ropes at the top of the pole were tied tightly to stakes in the ground. These ropes held the center pole firmly in place.

Another truck drove around the pole, unrolling sheets of tent material on the ground. Then workers laced all the tent sheets together to make one big tent, which was tied to the bale ring.

Rosie was harnessed to another rope that was tied to the bale ring. This time when Rosie pulled the rope, the bale ring began moving up the pole, raising the tent that was attached to it. When the tent was all the way up, Max clapped his hands. Next the tent was stretched tight, and then the side pieces were put on.

The Big Top was up!

Inside the Big Top, workers began putting together the seats for the audience.

Some workers unloaded props and equipment. Others ran cables and hung lights.

"The performers set up their own riggings to make sure they're safe," Grandpa Sam said. "There's Mary, a trapeze artist, pulling her trapeze bar up into the air."

Max watched some acrobats practice and listened to them talk about getting a new trick just right. He tried to turn a cartwheel, but he didn't quite land on his feet. Eduardo, a tumbler from Mexico, helped Max up.

"Just keep practicing," Eduardo said, laughing. "Practice is the secret."

Outside, Max saw a drinking trough being filled from the water truck.

"The animals are given water four times a day," the driver told him. "I have to make many trips to town every day to get enough water for the animals and the circus people."

Fresh food was also brought in from town. The animals needed hay, oats, bran, corn, lettuce, cabbage, carrots, onions, potatoes, celery, and meat.

Once the circus had been set up and the animals had been fed, it was time for the crew to eat.

Grandpa Sam and Max had lunch with some of Grandpa Sam's friends. They told stories about the old days. Circus people call this "jack potting." They told Max tales of beautiful hand-carved circus wagons, daredevil acts, and elephants that had run away to munch on tree leaves.

After lunch, Grandpa Sam walked Max to the back lot. This was the area behind the Big Top where the performers lived. Performers, trainers, and musicians were changing into their costumes and getting ready for the show.

Grandpa Sam learned something new when Felix the clown said that leotards were invented more than a hundred years ago by a French trapeze artist named Jules Leotard.

Sophie the seamstress told Max she had sewn thousands of sequins, rhinestones, and glass beads onto many of the costumes. "They make the costumes glitter and sparkle," she said.

Sophie showed Max huge headdresses made of ostrich feathers, which were dyed to match the colors of the costumes. Some of them were quite heavy!

Mr. Hanbury invited Max and Grandpa Sam over to Clown Alley. Max was amazed to see Mr. Hanbury become Bo the Clown! "Clowns put on their makeup very carefully," Mr. Hanbury said. "And no two clowns ever look alike."

"I make my own props," Mr. Hanbury told Max. "Look at my ladder. I put some rubber steps on it so it looks like I'm falling."

Chi Chi decided to make something for her costume, too.

People were beginning to line up for the show. Some of them stopped at the animal rides first.

Backstage, the performance director signaled the performers to line up for their entrance. Then she made sure that everyone was in the right place.

20

The grand entrance of the performers and animals was called the Spectacle or the Spec. "When the band starts playing, the performers know the show will soon begin," Grandpa Sam told Max.

After a few tunes, the band stopped playing and the ringmaster stepped into the arena. In a booming voice he announced: "Ladies and gentlemen and children, all. Welcome to the Boone-Rissler Family Circus! What a wonder and a joy is a circus parade!" Then the band started up again, and the Spec parade began.

Max knew the ringmaster was one of the most important people in the show. Grandpa Sam had told him that the ringmaster blows a whistle to begin and end each act and to tell the band when to play. Max was proud that his grandfather had been a ringmaster. He held Grandpa Sam's hand as they watched the Spec go by.

After the Spec, the performance began with Daring Dan and his dogs. Dan pretended not to know that Bow and Wow were taking his juggling pins. But that's just what he had trained them to do.

The Towering Tengs were acrobats who had come all the way from China.

Max noticed that some of the Bouncing Barretts were children like him. He asked Grandpa Sam how they got jobs with the circus. Sam explained that, like many circus acts, they came from a circus family. "Their parents and grandparents were in the circus before them," Sam said. "Jamie Barrett and his sisters, Valerie and Kristin, grew up around circus equipment and learned to use it when they were very young."

"That isn't the only way to get into the circus," said Grandpa Sam, pointing to the lion tamer. "Karen started at a circus taking care of the lions. Then she worked as an assistant to a wild-animal trainer for many years. She learned to train the lions. When the trainer went to another show, she took over the act. She got to be a star by working very hard."

"There are also schools," Grandpa Sam continued. "One circus has a special school for clowns."
Max wondered what it would be like to go to a circus school.

As the show came to an end, the lights went out and the arena became dark. Suddenly, shimmering colored lights came on, and the bareback rider rode out. Max thought her horse was the most beautiful one he had ever seen!

When the evening show was over, the workers began packing up. Tomorrow the circus would be moving to another town. After everything inside the tent had been removed, the rope that held the bale ring was untied. Max was sad to see the Big Top slowly slide down the center pole and drop to the ground.

Early the next morning, the circus drove off to another town. Max and Grandpa Sam came to wave good-bye to their friends. As they were leaving the empty circus lot, Grandpa Sam asked Max if he would like to work in the circus someday.

Max stopped. Then he ran and turned a perfect cartwheel . . . then another.

Do you want to know more about the circus? Here are some places where you can get more information.

Books:

Many books about the circus are available at public libraries. A recent book of photographs, called *Mud Show*, by Edwin Martin, is available from the University of New Mexico Press, Albuquerque, New Mexico 87131.

Organizations

Circus World Museum, Baraboo, Wisconsin 53913.

Circus Historical Society, Johann W. Dahlinger, 743 Beverly Park Place, Jackson, Michigan 49203. Publishes *The Bandwagon* magazine.

Circus Fans Association of America, J. Allen Duffield, P.O. Box 69, Camp Hill, Pennsylvania 17011. Publishes *The White Tops* magazine.

Circus Model Builders, Sally Conover Weitlauf, 347 Longsdale Avenue, Dayton, Ohio 45419. Publishes *The Little Circus Wagon* magazine.